This
Treasure Cove Story
belongs to

I AM THE GENIE

A CENTUM BOOK 978-1-913110-10-9
Published in Great Britain by Centum Books Ltd.
This edition published 2020.

1 3 5 7 9 10 8 6 4 2

Centum Books Ltd, 20 Devon Square, Newton Abbot,
Devon, TQ12 2HR, UK.

www.centumbooksltd.co.uk | books@centumbooksltd.co.uk
CENTUM BOOKS Limited Reg. No. 07641486.

A CIP catalogue record for this book is available
from the British Library.

Printed in China.

centum

Disney Aladdin

I Am the Genie

By John Sazaklis

Illustrated by Alan Batson

Greetings, friends!

I am the **Genie** of the lamp!

I am
BIG

and I am **blue**.

I can change **SHAPE** and **Size** and **hue**!

I have **POWERS** as GREAT as the **GALAXY**!

But I have an itty-bitty living space.

Being stuck in a
magic lamp gives me
such a **crick** in the neck!

My lamp is hidden in the **Cave of Wonders**.

It is found by two guests
in vests – a thief named
Aladdin and his monkey,
Abu. Aladdin rubs the
lamp and...

TA-DA!

Here I am!

Boy, does it **FEEL** good to be out of there!

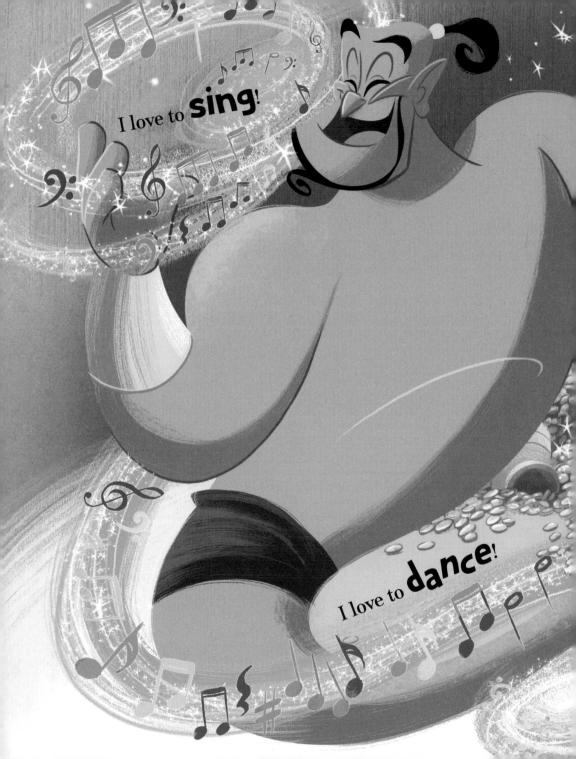

I love making
MAGIC
when given the chance.

No one's *ever* had
a **friend** like **me**!

As servant of the lamp, I can grant

3

wishes.

There are rules, though:

I can't hurt anyone.

I can't make anyone fall in love.

I can't bring anyone back to life.

*And no one is allowed to wish for more wishes.

Aladdin wishes to become a prince so he can go to Agrabah and win the **heart** of Princess Jasmine.

I have a *genie-us* idea.
He'll dress **to impress**!

And... **POOF!** The first **wish** is granted.

I make a
fancy-pants
prince...

and a **MIGHTY** monkey-elephant!

I *always* travel in **style**.
I lead Aladdin to the palace with

golden camels,

purple peacocks

and
llamas galore.

On a scale of ONE to TEN,
my entrance is an ELEVEN!
But Princess Jasmine is
not impressed.

I also give good advice.
I tell Aladdin,
'*BEE* YOURSELF!'

It's not what's on the outside,
but what's **on the inside** that counts.

I think a **magic carpet** ride will help Aladdin and Jasmine get to know each other...

and fall in **love**.

I was right, it does, and **they do!**

Thanks to me,
Aladdin is a
star!

By marrying the princess,
he will become the sultan one day.
But Jafar, the royal advisor, wants to
get rid of Aladdin and **take over**
the kingdom!

When Jafar throws my buddy into the ocean,
I **rush** to the rescue.

My loyalty saves Aladdin's life,
but the rescue comes with a price:
his second **wish**.

Aladdin and I make a terrific team.
With our **BRAVERY** and **CLEVERNESS**,
we outwit that wicked Jafar.

I turn Jafar into a genie.
He is trapped in a little lamp
FOREVER!

Aladdin tells Jasmine he is not really a prince. When she chooses to marry him anyway, my heart fills with **joy**.

And guess what?
Aladdin uses his final **wish**
to release me from my lamp.
Now I am **overjoyed**!

There's a **whole new world**
out there for me.

I am the **Genie** – and I am free!

Treasure Cove Stories

Please contact Centum Books
to receive the full list of titles in
the *Treasure Cove Stories* series.
books@centumbooksltd.co.uk

Classic favourites

1 Three Little Pigs
2 Snow White and
the Seven Dwarfs
3 The Fox and the Hound
- Hide-and-Seek
4 Dumbo
5 Cinderella
6 Cinderella's Friends
7 Alice in Wonderland
8 Mad Hatter's Tea Party
from Alice in Wonderland
9 Mickey Mouse and
his Spaceship
10 Peter Pan
11 Pinocchio
12 Mickey and the Beanstalk
13 Sleeping Beauty
and the Good Fairies
14 The Lucky Puppy
15 Chicken Little
16 The Incredibles
17 Coco
18 Winnie the Pooh and Tigger
19 The Sword in the Stone
20 Mary Poppins
21 The Jungle Book
22 The Aristocats
23 Lady and the Tramp
24 Bambi
25 Bambi - Friends of the Forest

Recently published

50 Frozen
51 Cinderella is my Babysitter
52 Beauty and the Beast
- I am the Beast
53 Blaze and the Monster Machines
- Mighty Monster Machines
54 Blaze and the Monster Machines
- Dino Parade!
55 Teenage Mutant Ninja Turtles
- Follow the Ninja!

56 I am a Princess
57 The Big Book of Paw Patrol
58 Paw Patrol
- Adventures with Grandpa!
59 Paw Patrol - Pirate Pups!
60 Trolls
61 Trolls Holiday
62 The Secret Life of Pets
63 Zootropolis
64 Ariel is my Babysitter
65 Tiana is my Babysitter
66 Belle is my Babysitter
67 Paw Patrol
- Itty-Bitty Kitty Rescue
68 Moana
69 Nella the Princess Knight
- My Heart is Bright!
70 Guardians of the Galaxy
71 Captain America
- High-Stakes Heist!
72 Ant-Man
73 The Mighty Avengers
74 The Mighty Avengers
- Lights Out!
75 The Incredible Hulk
76 Shimmer & Shine
- Wish Upon a Sleepover
77 Shimmer & Shine - Backyard Ballet
78 Paw Patrol - All-Star Pups!
79 Teenage Mutant Ninja Turtles
- Really Spaced Out!
80 I am Ariel
81 Madagascar
82 Jasmine is my Babysitter
83 How to Train your Dragon
84 Shrek
85 Puss in Boots
86 Kung Fu Panda
87 Beauty and the Beast - I am Belle
88 The Lion Guard
- The Imaginary Okapi
89 Thor - Thunder Strike!
90 Guardians of the Galaxy
- Rocket to the Rescue!
91 Nella the Princess Knight
- Nella and the Dragon
92 Shimmer & Shine
- Treasure Twins!

93 Olaf's Frozen Adventure
94 Black Panther
95 Trolls
- Branch's Bunker Birthday
96 Trolls - Poppy's Party
97 The Ugly Duckling
98 Cars - Look Out for Mater!
99 101 Dalmatians
100 The Sorcerer's Apprentice
101 Tangled
102 Avengers
- The Threat of Thanos
103 Puppy Dog Pals
- Don't Rain on my Pug-Rade
104 Jurassic Park
105 The Mighty Thor
106 Doctor Strange

Latest publications

107 Captain Marvel
108 The Invincible Iron Man
109 Black Panther
- Warriors of Wakanda
110 The Big Freeze
111 Ratatouille
112 Aladdin
113 Aladdin - I am the Genie
114 Seven Dwarfs Find a House
115 Toy Story
116 Toy Story 4
117 Paw Patrol - Jurassic Bark!
118 Paw Patrol
- Mighty Pup Power!
119 Shimmer & Shine
- Pet Talent Show!
120 SpongeBob SquarePants
- Krabby Patty Caper
121 The Lion King - I am Simba
122 Winnie the Pooh
- The Honey Tree
123 Frozen II
124 Baby Shark and the
Colours of the Ocean
125 Baby Shark and
the Police Sharks!
126 Trolls World Tour

Book list may be subject to change.